NC

D0198696

SCOUT and ACE

Three Heads to Feed

Written by Rose Impey
Illustrated by Ant Parker

ORCHARD BOOKS

Once upon a time, our heroes,

SCOUT and **ACE**

set out on a trip

into outer, outer-space.

Sucked through a worm-hole . . .

to a strange, new place,

lost in a galaxy called Fairy Tale Space.

"Check this out," says Scout. "That's one sad little face," says Ace.

It's an S.O.S from the planet Trigonia.

Scout and Ace race to the rescue.

But when they step out of the SuperStar . . .

. . . they step straight into a trap. SNAP!

"I am Trigon, Lord of all Trigonia! Raghhh!" roars the ogre.

All three heads at once.

The ogre locks Scout
and Ace in a cell.
They bang on the bars
and start to yell.

But the ogre plans to fatten them up. He brings them lots of food to eat.

But Ace has a plan too. "We're not scared of you," he tells the ogre. "What can you do?"

This makes the ogre mad.
He turns red in the face. All three
of them.
"I'll show you what I can do,"
he growls.

Flit-flit-Flat!

The ogre turns into
a giant vampire bat.

"That's what I can do!"
roars the ogre.

Pit - a - Pit - a - Pat!

The ogre turns into a rat.

But Ace, being a cat . . .

. . . soon catches that.

"Another brilliant plan of mine!" says Ace, as they head back to the SuperStar.

"Did you hear about the three-headed ogre who went on strike for more pay?" says Ace. "He had two extra mouths to feed. Boom! Boom!"

Scout groans.
"Time to get out of here."

Fire the engines...

and lower the dome.

Once more our heroes...

are heading for home.

Enjoy all these stories about

SCOUT and ACE

and their adventures in Space!

Hardbacks priced at £8.99 each..

Colour Crunchies are available from all good bookshops, or can be ordered direct from the publisher:
Orchard Books, PO BOX 29, Douglas MM99 1BQ.
Credit card orders please telephone 01624 836000 or fax 01624 837033
or email: *bookshop@enterprise.net* for details.

To order please quote title, author and ISBN and your full name and address. Cheques and postal
orders should be made payable to 'Bookpost plc'. Postage and packing is FREE within the UK –
overseas customers should add £1.00 per book. Prices and availability are subject to change.

ORCHARD BOOKS, 96 Leonard Street, London EC2A 4XD.
Hachette Children's Books, Level 17/207 Kent Street, Sydney, NSW 2000.
This edition first published in Great Britain in hardback in 2005. First paperback publication 2006.
Text © Rose Impey 2005. Illustrations © Ant Parker 2005. The rights of Rose Impey to be identified as
the author and Ant Parker to be identified as the illustrator have been asserted by them in accordance with the
Copyright, Designs and Patents Act, 1988. A CIP catalogue record for this book is available from the British Library
ISBN 1 84362 169 X (hardback)   10 9 8 7 6 5 4 3 2 1
Printed in China